Maddy Lou & Mack

at the
STATE FAIR of TEXAS

Krystal Granzow

Illustrated by
Alvina Kwong

BROWN BOOKS KIDS

Maddy Lou & Mack at the State Fair of Texas

Brown Books Kids
16250 Knoll Trail Drive, Suite 205
Dallas, Texas 75248
www.BrownBooksKids.com
(972) 381-0009

A New Era in Publishing®

ISBN 978-1-61254-961-3
LCCN 2017932161

Printed in the United States
10 9 8 7 6 5 4 3 2 1

The marks STATE FAIR OF TEXAS®, BIG TEX®, TEXAS STATE FAIR®, and the Big Tex Image® are federally registered to and property of the State Fair of Texas.

For more information or to contact the author, please go to www.KrystalGranzow.com.

Dedication

For Kyle Mack, my breathtaking baby boy.

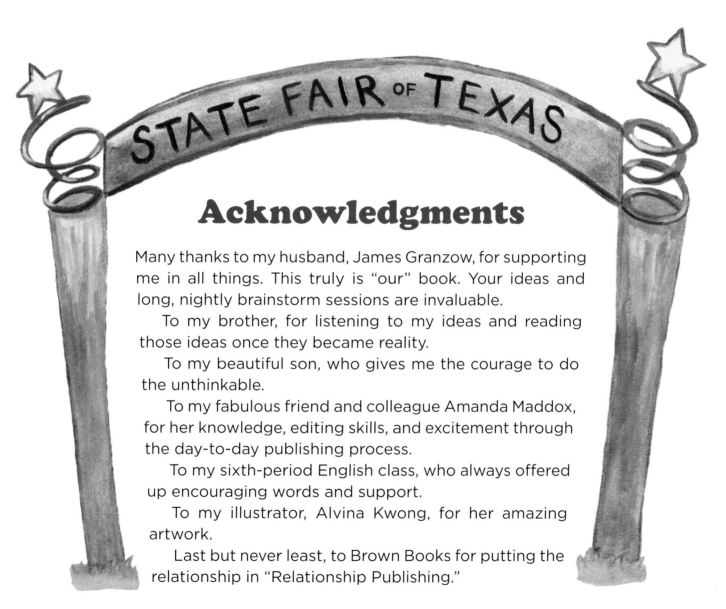

Acknowledgments

Many thanks to my husband, James Granzow, for supporting me in all things. This truly is "our" book. Your ideas and long, nightly brainstorm sessions are invaluable.

To my brother, for listening to my ideas and reading those ideas once they became reality.

To my beautiful son, who gives me the courage to do the unthinkable.

To my fabulous friend and colleague Amanda Maddox, for her knowledge, editing skills, and excitement through the day-to-day publishing process.

To my sixth-period English class, who always offered up encouraging words and support.

To my illustrator, Alvina Kwong, for her amazing artwork.

Last but never least, to Brown Books for putting the relationship in "Relationship Publishing."

Maddy Lou and her big brother, Mack, make many memories together as they take trips.

They love to learn about Texas.

The weather is always nice in Texas.

Sometimes, Maddy Lou and Mack wear shorts.

At other times,
they wear jackets.

Every year in the month of October, Maddy Lou and Mack visit the State Fair of Texas. There are only twenty-four days to visit the fair.

Big brother Mack exclaims, "The State Fair started as a small gathering in 1886. Back then, they called it the Dallas State Fair."

Maddy Lou happily replies, "I'm glad they chose to name it the State Fair of Texas instead."

On their visits to the fair each year,

Maddy Lou and Mack always stop to see

BIG TEX.

Before visiting Big Tex, Maddy Lou and Mack must have their favorite Fletcher's corn dog.

The Fletcher brothers started selling corn dogs at the State Fair of Texas in 1942. Each year, Fletcher's sells thousands of corn dogs.

"Howdy, y'all!" proudly proclaims Big Tex.

Maddy Lou and Mack learn that Big Tex is fifty-five feet tall.

Big Tex made his first appearance at the State Fair in 1952.

Maddy Lou and Mack have their parents take a picture of them with Big Tex.

Afterward, Maddy Lou and Mack hurry to their favorite part of the fair, the Texas Star Ferris Wheel.

This large Ferris wheel is the biggest in Texas. Maddy Lou and Mack ride the wheel at night, when it is lit up like a Christmas tree. They love looking far, far away over the Dallas sky.

"Well, Maddy Lou, our fun day is over.
I guess it's time to go home," states Mack.

Maddy Lou and Mack have had a terrific
time at the State Fair of Texas.

Mack asks his best friend, "Where will we go next, Maddy Lou?"

On to our next amazing adventure!

About the Author

Krystal Granzow is a certified secondary English language arts teacher and holds a master's degree in educational leadership. Since 2009, she has worked with youth in an educational setting, using alliteration as a tool to help give children access to higher-level vocabulary and enhance their writing skills. She now lives in Lubbock, Texas, with her husband, Jimmy, her son, Kyle Mack, and her big little brother, John Dakota. Krystal grew up ritually spending "fair days" at Fair Park with her mom, which in part inspired her to write her first children's book about the State Fair of Texas. When she's not teaching freshman English, she enjoys reading, hiking, spending time with family, and all things Texas.

About the Illustrator

Alvina Kwong was born in Hawaii and moved to Southern California when she was about seven years old. She loves the ocean, dogs, and ice cream. The minute she started to draw her first unicorn, she knew that the pencil was a magical wand and the ticket to her imagination. She graduated from Brigham Young University with a BFA in illustration and currently lives in Los Angeles with her family and goofy boxer. Visit AlvinaKwong.Blogspot.com for more of her art and books.